The Country Pancake

Also by Anne Fine

How to Write Really Badly
The Country Pancake
The Angel of Nitshill Road
'The chicken gave it to me'
Anneli the Art Hater
Press Play
Scaredy Cat
Countdown
Design a Pram
A Sudden Puff of Glittering Smoke
A Sudden Swirl of Icy Wind
A Sudden Glow of Gold

Telling Tales – An Interview with Anne Fine

For older readers
The Summer House Loon
The Other Darker Ned
The Granny Project
The Stone Menagerie
Very Different

Anne Fine
Children's Laureate

The Country Pancake

EGMONT

You can visit Anne Fine's website,
www.annefine.co.uk, and download gorgeous
free bookplates from www.myhomelibrary.org

First published in Great Britain 1989
by Methuen Children's Books Ltd
Reissued 2002 by Egmont Books Ltd
239 Kensington High Street
London W8 6SA

Text copyright © 1989 Anne Fine
Inside illustrations copyright © 1989 Philippe Dupasquier
Cover illustration copyright © 2002 Lee Gibbons

The moral rights of the author and illustrators
have been asserted

ISBN 1 4052 0062 6

10 9 8 7 6 5 4 3

A CIP catalogue record for this title is
available from the British Library

Printed and bound by Cox & Wyman Ltd
Reading, Berkshire

Contents

Chapter 1

**In which we are introduced to
Lancelot, Miss Mirabelle and
Flossie the Cow**

Lance sat on the wooden fence that ran round
the meadow, watching the cows and worrying
as usual about his teacher, Miss Mirabelle.
Two feet away, Flossie his favourite burped
gently, flicked her long raggedy tail, and
watched him anxiously.

'It's no good, Flossie,' said Lance. 'Things
aren't getting better. They are getting *worse*.'

Flossie shook her big heavy head and
looked, if possible, even more anxious

than before.

'If she's not careful,' Lance warned, 'she's going to lose her job. She'll get the sack. Why, she spent almost half an hour this morning just staring out of the window sucking her pencil. There was practically a riot at the back of the classroom.'

Flossie turned round and ambled off towards the ragged bit of fence that was so good for back-scratching.

Left to himself, Lance sighed and stared up at the vast bowl of sky.

'She ought to try to do better,' he told the clouds above him. 'She's always writing it on other people's reports. She ought to try it herself. She should pull her socks up. She should get a grip. We can't go on like this. It's beyond a joke.'

Behind him another cow burped, rather more rudely than Flossie.

'All right for *you*.' Lance scowled. 'You never had to go to school. You don't know what it can be like.'

The Country Pancake

Lance remembered only too well what school was like before Miss Mirabelle came. First there was Mr Rushman. Terrifying! He spoke so softly you could hardly hear, and then, as soon as you did something wrong because you hadn't heard, he shouted at you that you ought to listen. No one was sorry when he left the school.

Then there was Mrs Maloney. She seemed to think they were all idiots. She spoke so loud and clear and slow, and said everything she had to say at least a dozen times, and everything they did was so easy-peasy that everyone was driven half mad with boredom. There was great relief all round when Mrs Maloney moved back down to Infants.

Then there was Mr Hubert. He talked all the time. Nobody else got a word in edgeways. They never did anything. They just watched him talk. He talked about what they were going to do, but took so long talking they never did it. Then he broke both legs falling off his motorbike. They all signed the card to the hospital, but nobody cried. They just felt a little bit sorry for the nurses.

And then, like an angel, Miss Mirabelle came. One morning they were all fiddling about at their tables or hanging around the windowsills wondering who was going to take them, when in stepped a vision in a flowery dress, with golden hair piled high and tumbling down, and silver bell earrings that tinkled as she moved, and scarlet fingernails and bare brown legs. And on her dainty feet the vision wore the brightest, greenest shoes, with frills round the edges and bows on top, and the highest heels ever seen at Wallisdean Park School.

'I am Miss Mirabelle,' the vision said. 'Get off those windowsills. Stop fiddling about. Plonk your bums straight down on your little chairs, and listen to me.'

Extraordinary!

Half the class slid off the windowsills and crept to their seats. The other half stopped fiddling. There was absolute silence.

The Country Pancake

You could have heard a pin drop. Everyone stared, wide-eyed and open-mouthed, as Miss Mirabelle hitched up her flowery skirts, perched on the very edge of the teacher's desk, crossed her legs elegantly at the knee, and told them:

'I am your new teacher, and I think I should tell you right at the start that I can stand practically anything in the world, but I can't stand *sniffers*.'

She reached in her capacious woven bag and pulled out a huge box of paper tissues.

'I'll put these here,' she said.

She placed the box ceremoniously on the front of her desk.

'At the first sign of a sniff, or a snuffle, or even a bit of a blocked nose, you are to come up here, take a tissue, and *blow*!'

She rose dramatically, and pointed to the cupboard at the back of the classroom.

'Sniffers will be sent to sit in there, out of sight and out of hearing. I'm sorry, but there it is. I just can't help it. Sniffers bring out the

Anne Fine

The Country Pancake

murderess in me.'

Then suddenly she smiled, picked up the chalk, and, swinging round, began to write the date very neatly on the blackboard, just like any other teacher in the world.

Her back safely turned, everyone took the chance to glance at their friends, and nudge their neighbours. Deborah even whispered to Lance.

'What do you think of her?'

'She's different.' Lance shook his head. 'She certainly is different.'

And he was right. Miss Mirabelle certainly was different. She started the school day with a Wake You Up Sing Song. Her silver bell earrings tinkled when she laughed. And every so often during the morning she reached into her capacious woven bag and, pulling out an exquisite little pearl knife and an apple, she peeled off the skin in one long perfect coil, sliced up the apple thinly, and popped each delicate sliver into her perfect red mouth.

Lance watched. It made a change, he

thought, from watching teachers mark books, or go round the class, or write on the board. Miss Mirabelle was different, she was exotic, she promised adventure. Lance longed for adventure, and he hoped she would stay.

But would she be able to stay different? Lance wasn't sure. He'd seen the headmistress take Miss Mirabelle aside after lunch, pointing first at Miss Mirabelle's high heels, then at the wooden floor in the hall. Mrs Spicer was worrying about pockmarks on her nice boards.

That's it for the shoes, then, thought Lance sadly. He knew Mrs Spicer's little talks. Mrs Spicer was a dragon. The high heels would end up in the bottom of Miss Mirabelle's closet. Tomorrow she'd be in flatties, or clumpies, like all the other teachers.

But she wasn't. The next day the amazing Miss Mirabelle turned up in the very same shoes.

The whisper ran round like wildfire.

'Wait till Mrs Spicer sees!'

The Country Pancake

Lance peeped at Miss Mirabelle. She didn't look worried. Cheerfully she called them into line and marched them smartly down the corridor towards the hall. But what would happen when Mrs Spicer saw her sail through the big swing doors wearing the same fancy shoes? Would Miss Mirabelle be told off? Sent out? Ordered home?

Lance was a bag of nerves. He imagined Mrs Spicer glancing up from her song book as the clatter of high heels came closer and closer along the corridor. He imagined her face darkening and her mouth drawing as tight as a purse string. He imagined her look of rage as Miss Mirabelle stepped on her precious wooden floor.

He was so nervous he would have liked to close his eyes as they went through the swing doors. Good thing he had to look to see where he was going. For otherwise he would have missed the sight of the amazing Miss Mirabelle reaching down, delicately flipping off first one shoe, then the other, and dangling them elegantly from her fingertips as she picked her way barefoot across the hall, settled herself neatly on her canvas chair, looked up and smiled.

Mrs Spicer was livid. She was so furious she got the title of the song mixed up. She was so furious she lost her place twice in the prayer. She was so furious she stumbled on her clumpy shoes on her way out of the hall,

The Country Pancake

leaving a scuff mark on her precious floor.

Miss Mirabelle smiled. Then she turned sweetly to her class.

'Come along, then,' she said. 'I think the show is over. Time to start on the work now.'

And that was another thing – the work. Work with Miss Mirabelle was different, too. Sometimes, when they were all doing something together, Miss Mirabelle would suddenly sigh, and complain:

'This is so boring. I am very bored.'

Often the class agreed. Someone would ask:

'Why do we do it, then?'

Miss Mirabelle would roll her eyes, and shrug.

'If you don't, you might grow up ignorant. I suppose being ignorant is even more boring than doing this.'

Sometimes they argued with her.

'This isn't boring.'

'It's not boring at all.'

'I'm really interested.'

'I could do this *all day*.'

Miss Mirabelle never minded them arguing. (That was another thing that made her different.) Sometimes she'd sit back and listen to what they had to say. Sometimes she'd look amazed, as if they were a pack of lunatics. Sometimes she'd simply lose interest, cup her head on her hands, and stare out of the window while the discussion turned into a riot around her.

Oh, she took some getting used to, did Miss Mirabelle. Admittedly she was nowhere near as terrifying as Mr Rushman, or as boring as Mrs Maloney, or as fond of her own voice as Mr Hubert. But she could certainly make them all jump. For one thing, she'd lied to them right at the start. She'd said she could stand practically anything in the world except sniffers, but it just wasn't true. There were a million things she couldn't stand. Hardly a day went by when Lance did not lean over the fence on his way home from school and, patting Flossie till the dust flew up in clouds, tell her:

The Country Pancake

'Miss Mirabelle can't *stand* people who lick their fingers before they turn over the pages of a book.'

Or:

'Miss Mirabelle can't *stand* people who snigger when someone says they have to go to the lavatory.'

Or:

'Miss Mirabelle can't *stand* people who fuss when a wasp flies in the classroom.'

Whatever it was Miss Mirabelle couldn't stand, Flossie would look as concerned as usual. Pushing her great head closer, she'd almost butt poor Lance off the fence.

'She hasn't much patience,' Lance confessed. 'She shouldn't really be a teacher. She's not quite right for the job. She went berserk when I forgot my gym shoes. She went mad when Deborah bent down the corner of her page, to mark her place. She took a fit when Ally dropped pencil sharpenings on the floor.'

He scratched Flossie's ears as hard as he

could, to please her. Her hide was so tough that it was hard work.

'I'm not sure she'll keep the job,' he said sadly. 'Not if she doesn't change her attitude . . .'

The idea of Miss Mirabelle leaving filled him with gloom. He'd suffered Mr Rushman, and Mrs Maloney, and Mr Hubert. He knew what school could be like.

It was as if Flossie wanted to shake him out of his black mood. She tossed her head, throwing poor Lance off balance once again.

'Really,' Lance insisted. 'Mrs Spicer has been suspicious of Miss Mirabelle ever since that business of the high-heeled shoes. She watches her terribly closely. Miss Mirabelle is in danger.'

He patted Flossie's flank and, not for the first time, wished with all his heart that Flossie had been born, not a cow, but a horse. Lance longed for a horse. He longed for adventure. He longed for unknown countries he could ride across, and dragons he could fight, and

damsels in distress he could rescue. Oh, Lance loved Flossie. Of course he did. He'd loved her since he first saw her, twenty minutes old, lying in deep straw, steaming, with damp and curly hair, and the farmer said: 'Choose a name,' and Lance called out: 'Flossie!'

Then he had sat on the wooden bars of the cow stall and watched as Big Buttercup licked her lovely newborn calf. After a bit, little Flossie began to struggle to her feet. Lance held his breath, willing her on. She tried so hard. Her spindly legs wobbled, letting her down time and again. But in the end she made it. Lance was thrilled. And with a bit of nudging from Big Buttercup's huge soft nose, the hungry little creature found the teat, wrapped her tongue around to get a grip, and sucked hard.

Lance went back day after day, to watch Flossie grow. He carried water and shovelled cow-cake for all the cattle on the farm, but Flossie was his favourite. He talked to her while she sniffed curiously at his pockets and butted him with her head to try and make him play, and followed him round the field. He told her everything, and kept on telling as the months went by, and Flossie grew and grew, till finally she was vast, enormous, bigger than Lance, almost as big as a car, with huge brown, anxious, motherly eyes.

So Lance loved her dearly. He always would. But she was only a cow. Cows weren't exotic. They weren't different. And they didn't promise adventure. You couldn't go righting

The Country Pancake

wrongs, killing dragons, rescuing damsels in distress with a cow. Let's face it, cows aren't even very bright.

Oh, Lance could still tell all his troubles to Flossie. She was still perfect for that. But it would be foolish to expect any more.

He took the shortcut home across the meadow, jumping the big brown cowpats and singing the song his friends always sang when somebody careless put their foot in one.

Which would you rather?

Run a mile,

Jump a stile,

Or eat a country pancake?

He wasn't daft. Though he was hungry now, and ready for tea, he'd run the mile or jump the stile!

Chapter 2

**In which Miss Mirabelle
tells a Giant Whopper**

Lance knew he was right to fear that Miss Mirabelle was in danger. You could tell from the look on Mrs Spicer's face that she was suspicious of her new teacher. She didn't like the way Miss Mirabelle made no effort to hide her yawns during assembly. She didn't like the fresh flowers Miss Mirabelle wore in her hair. She gave them such a poisonous look that Lance couldn't help expecting them to wilt. She put a firm stop to Miss Mirabelle's Wake

The Country Pancake

You Up Sing Songs and frowned when she heard the high heels clattering down the corridor.

And sometimes she made surprise visits to the classroom. (She'd never done that before, even when Mr Rushman was terrifying them half to death, or Mrs Maloney was boring them stupid, or Mr Hubert's endless nattering was getting on their nerves.) She'd creep along the corridors, making no sound. Suddenly her head would appear behind the little square pane of glass set in the door.

Everyone's eyes would swivel round. Miss Mirabelle would notice at once.

'Fancy!' she'd say. 'A visitor! How very refreshing. We do welcome breaks.'

The door would open. Mrs Spicer would creep in, rubbing her hands.

'Don't let me interrupt you, Miss Mirabelle. I'll wait till you've finished. Please carry on, *exactly* as before.'

Miss Mirabelle would smile her sweet smile, and turn back to the class.

'Where was I?' she'd ask.

Then, before anyone could tell her that she'd been admiring Melissa's tooth which was hanging only by a thread, or showing them photographs of her sister's wedding, or asking their advice on a name for her new kitten, she'd carry on, very firmly indeed:

'Oh, yes. As I was just saying, it's time to get out your workbooks and carry on, while I come round the class.'

She'd turn to Mrs Spicer, and spread her hands.

'Now,' she'd say angelically. 'How can I help you?'

She didn't always get away with it so easily. Mrs Spicer found sniffers in the cupboard several times, and wasn't very pleased. The whole class was spotted through the windows one day with their eyes firmly closed, after Miss Mirabelle discovered that rubbing her eyes very gently made a faint squelch. And then there were all the times Mrs Spicer walked past the room and, glancing in quickly, caught

The Country Pancake

Miss Mirabelle with her head propped on her hands, staring out of the window while such a riot went on around her that no one even noticed the spy in the doorway.

Mrs Spicer would fling the door open.

'Miss Mirabelle?'

Everyone noticed her now. There was absolute quiet.

'Miss Mirabelle!' she'd call again, even more sharply.

Miss Mirabelle would give herself a little shake, and turn around slowly.

'Oh!'

She'd look astonished, as if it were not possible that she was really still sitting here in the classroom, with so many children around her. 'Sorry. I must have been miles away. I was having a daydream.'

And Mrs Spicer would close the door with a fierce little bang, to let Miss Mirabelle know that a classroom was no place for a daydream.

But Miss Mirabelle wasn't the only one to

The Country Pancake

suffer from daydreams. Lance spent hours staring into space, wondering how he could protect Miss Mirabelle from danger. He suspected Mrs Spicer of spending her days locked in her office secretly writing letters of complaint about Miss Mirabelle to important people.

Dear Head of the Governors,
Miss Mirabelle does not fit in at Wallisdean Park School. She hasn't the right attitude. Her clothes are too fancy, and her heels are too high. She spends far too much time staring out of the window, and holds eye-squelching sessions when she is bored.
On her very own admission, sniffers bring out the **murderess** *in her. I think she ought to go.*
Yours truly,
Emily Spicer

Lost in his daydreams, Lance thought what he'd do. He'd run like the very wind down to the meadow, where Flossie would be standing, her head lowered, cropping the fresh juicy grasses. But Flossie was strangely altered in his daydream. Her legs and neck were longer. Her body was nowhere near as bulky as usual. Muscles rippled beneath her glossy skin. Her head was a different shape. Only the lovely velvet-brown eyes remained the same. The rest of Flossie had become a beautiful and fleet-footed horse who whinnied with excitement and promised adventure.

Lance would scale the fence. Flossie would prance closer. Lance would make a flying leap on to her back, and she would clear the fence with a jump so high and wide and smooth and effortless, it was like flying.

He'd clutch her silken mane as they gathered speed along the country lane. Her delicate hooves would clatter as they spun along. Her tail would fly out behind.

But Mrs Spicer would be almost at the letterbox, her tell-tale letter in her outstretched hand. Would they be in time to rescue Miss Mirabelle?

The Country Pancake

Yes! Quicker than a lightning flash, Flossie would canter through. Hanging on to her mane for dearest life, Lance would lean down, and, reaching out, snatch the offending letter from the old dragon's hand.

'You *shan't* get rid of Miss Mirabelle!' he'd cry bravely. 'I shall save her!'

And ripping the mean little letter into a thousand pieces, he'd scatter it to the four winds as they rode home.

If only life itself were that simple! The weeks of term went by. Everyone's workbook filled up, and everyone moved on to a different-coloured reader. Miss Mirabelle certainly made them all work. But still Lance couldn't help worrying about her. It seemed to him that he couldn't walk down a corridor without seeing Mrs Spicer purse her lips, or raise her eyebrows, or give a cold little look of disapproval as the amazing Miss Mirabelle sailed by.

'It's getting worse,' he warned Flossie gloomily. 'Mrs Spicer is definitely out to get

The Country Pancake

her. You wait and see.'

And Flossie didn't have to wait long. It wasn't more than another week before Lance came home from school one day dragging his feet, with his head hanging.

Flossie picked her way through the mud in the ditch and stuck her head over the wooden fence to greet him.

Lance took no notice. He just kept walking.

Flossie let out a loud, long, plaintive moo.

Lance turned and, noticing Flossie for the first time that afternoon, hurried back to climb the fence and slide his arms around her neck.

'Oh, Flossie!' he said. 'Guess what has happened.'

Flossie looked anxious.

'Miss Mirabelle has been so silly. She's in big trouble.'

Flossie pulled a hoof out of the mud with a great sucking sound, then put it back in exactly the same place.

Lance explained.

'You see, it's nearly Open Day, when each class does something special to make a bit of money.'

Flossie tilted her head.

'People from other classes keep coming up to us,' explained Lance, 'and asking, "What is your class doing this year?"'

He looked dismayed.

'And we can't *answer*.'

He spread his hands.

'Miss Mirabelle won't *choose*,' he told Flossie. 'She won't admit it, but I think she thinks the whole idea of making money is boring. She's very easily bored. So she keeps putting off the decision. We never *choose*.'

He patted Flossie on the neck, more to comfort himself than to comfort the cow.

'Everyone else chose *weeks* ago,' he said. 'Class One is going to run a little Bring and buy stall. Class Two is putting on a show in the hall. Class Three has organised a sponsored run. Even the Infants are making Spaceman Snoopy collecting boxes out of old

The Country Pancake

toilet roll holders and bits of tinfoil.'

He paused, sunk in gloom.

'And we've done *nothing*!'

Flossie rubbed her massive head against the fence. Clouds of dust flew up in Lance's face, but he was so preoccupied he didn't notice.

'And that's not the worst of it,' he told Flossie. 'Mrs Spicer has been popping in every day to ask Miss Mirabelle, "Have you decided yet?" And Miss Mirabelle just keeps answering, "No, not quite yet." You can tell Mrs Spicer is getting terribly suspicious. You see, she doesn't like Miss Mirabelle's attitude.'

He shook his head. Flossie shook hers.

'And this morning,' he told Flossie, 'Mrs Spicer lost her patience and stormed into our room. You could tell she was on the war-path. She asked Miss Mirabelle again.'

Flossie's huge, loving, brown eyes were melting.

'And Miss Mirabelle panicked, and told a lie! "Oh, yes," she said. "That's all fixed up now." '

Flossie blinked twice.

'Quite,' agreed Lance. 'A bare-faced lie! And Mrs Spicer didn't believe it, either. She saw us all sitting with our mouths open, and she asked Miss Mirabelle, as sweet as sugared poison, "And may I ask what, exactly, your class has decided to do?" '

Lance's face paled as he told his dear Flossie the worst of it.

'And Miss Mirabelle replied, "I'm afraid I can't tell you, Mrs Spicer. You see, it's a secret." '

Flossie let out a soft bellow of amazement.

'That's right,' said Lance. 'Miss Mirabelle told a giant whopper. She has no secret plan. She can't have. She doesn't have a plan at all!'

He slid down from the fence on Flossie's side, to take the shortcut home across the meadow.

'And with only just over a week left, she's not very likely to think of one, is she?' he added bitterly.

The Country Pancake

Shades of the terrifying Mr Rushman and the boring Mrs Maloney rose up to haunt him. Perhaps even the dreaded Mr Hubert's broken legs had healed by now.

'We have to save her, Flossie!' he announced. 'We *must* save Miss Mirabelle from the dragon Spicer!'

On his way home, absorbed by anxiety and gloom, he put his foot right in a pancake.

Chapter 3

**In which the
Terrible, Terrible Secret
hangs heavily over All**

Miss Mirabelle came into school next morning in the worst mood. The clattering of her high heels coming closer down the corridor sounded as dangerous as machine-gun fire. She slammed the door shut behind her, hurled her capacious woven bag on to her desk, then put her hands on her hips.

She glowered round the class.

'Start thinking about this Open Day,' she told them.

The Country Pancake

Start thinking? What a *cheek*! Lance practically needed two matchsticks to keep his eyes propped open. He was exhausted. *Start* thinking? He'd been lying awake thinking all night!

'I thought you already had a plan,' Deborah said, mystified. 'You told Mrs Spicer it was all fixed up. You said it was a secret.'

The faintest blush rose on Miss Mirabelle's cheeks.

'I did have a bit of an idea,' she said, embarrassed. 'And, at the time, it seemed better to keep it a secret. But it wasn't much of an idea. And now I've forgotten it.'

She glanced round, as though daring them not to believe her.

'At least we've still got a secret,' giggled Deborah. 'It is a secret that we've got no plan.

Miss Mirabelle wasn't amused. Sinking on to her chair, she buried her head in her hands.

'Oh, it's certainly a secret: a terrible, terrible secret. It's been hanging over me all night.'

And me, Lance thought privately.

Anne Fine

Miss Mirabelle raised her head.

'Think,' she told all of them. 'We don't have much time. Think very *hard*.'

They all sat thinking hard. Every few minutes someone would shoot up a hand and make a suggestion. But no one came up with an idea Lance hadn't already thought of, and given up, because it was impossible –

'We could hire elephants from the zoo!'

Or another class was already doing it –

'We could put on a little show in the hall!'

Or it would take more than a week to organise –

'We could invite somebody famous, and sell tickets!'

The ideas were all hopeless. Miss Mirabelle got more and more miserable. She reached in her capacious woven bag and took out her little pearl knife and an apple. For the first time ever her hands shook a little as she peeled, so that her usual perfect coil fell off in ragged chunks.

The class watched silently. They'd seen

Miss Mirabelle bored, and they'd seen her cross-patch. They'd never seen her rattled. It made them nervous.

'Surely,' she kept saying, 'One of you can think of *something*.'

It seemed to Lance that she was looking directly at him.

But no one could think of anything. The morning went from bad to worse. Miss Mirabelle fell into an even blacker mood. She was snapping at people for everything they did, then snapping at them for not doing anything. And she threatened Deborah with the cupboard for just breathing loudly, nothing like sniffing at all! After a bit Lance found himself beginning to wonder whether Miss Mirabelle deserved to be rescued. It was her own fault, after all. She should never have wasted all that time staring out of the window, or told that foolish Giant Whopper.

But he couldn't help wanting to help her, all the same. She was still the amazing Miss Mirabelle. She stood there in her brilliant yellow dress with golden sunflowers sewn on with gleaming beads. She was so exotic, so different (and so much of an improvement on Mr Rushman and Mrs Maloney, and the dreadful Mr Hubert). He couldn't help wanting to save her. He knew what school could be like.

And her black mood did not last long.

'Come on,' she said, after a while. 'Worrying is so *boring*. Let's have a change. Let's do some painting. You can all think while you paint, and we'll do our work later.'

She went to the cupboard and wheeled out the trolley with all the art supplies.

Lance took his sheet of paper and a brush. Flattening the paper in front of him, he stabbed his paintbrush into the first paint pot Miss Mirabelle handed him and took a look. It was bright green.

Without thinking, he swept his brush over the paper. And again . . . And again . . . The green was very green. It was like grass after a week of sun and showers. Lance drifted gently off into a daydream. Together, he and Flossie were pounding over the lush green grass of the meadow. They were off on an adventure – crossing the world to right wrongs, kill dragons, rescue damsels in distress.

He was paying no attention at all to his painting. He didn't even bother to change colours. He just kept sticking his brush into the pot in front of him. Gradually the whole sheet of paper was filling up green.

Just as he was imagining sweeping Miss

Mirabelle up beside him on Flossie's strong back, out of the reach of the dragon, she surprised him by appearing in the flesh at his shoulder.

'What's that?' she asked, pointing.

Lance took a look at what he'd done. It was a sheet of paper painted green. That's all there was.

'It's a meadow,' Lance said quickly. (It was the only green thing that sprang to mind.)

Miss Mirabelle wasn't impressed.

'Real meadows don't look like that,' she scoffed. 'Real meadows aren't just solid green squares. They have weeds, and patches of mud, and fences and ditches. They have molehills and paths across them. And wild flowers, and cows.'

She sailed off, to look at someone else's work.

Lance scowled at her departing back. Really, when she was in this mood she wasn't a damsel worth rescuing at all.

'And cowpats,' he added rudely under his

breath. 'Don't forget they have cowpats.'

And, reaching across, he stuck his paintbrush into one of the other pots, stabbed at his plain green square, and ground the brush round and round.

'There!' he said crossly. 'A real meadow.'

A splotch of cowpat brown sat right in the middle of his sheet of paper. One country pancake in a field of green.

Lance stared at it. And then he stared some more. Then some more. Inside his brain, a little idea was growing, growing, growing.

An idea that grew, like Flossie the baby calf, until it was enormous. An idea big enough to save the day.

'Miss Mirabelle.'

Lance tiptoed towards her desk. She was sitting with her head cupped in her hands, staring out of the window.

'Miss Mirabelle,' he whispered. 'I have had an idea.'

Miss Mirabelle turned her head.

'An idea?'

She looked hopeful.

'Yes,' Lance said softly. 'I have an idea. It's easy to arrange, and no one else would ever think of doing it.'

Her eyes lit up. Could it be possible?

'And,' Lance added proudly, 'it is exactly the sort of idea that really ought to be kept a secret.'

Miss Mirabelle's velvety-brown eyes were melting as she looked at him.

'Tell me,' she said. Excitedly, she pushed the box of tissues aside and patted the corner of

The Country Pancake

her desk. 'Sit here and tell me your idea.'

'It's very *different*,' warned Lance. 'Some people might even think it was –' He paused, searching for the right word, and couldn't find it. He finished up: '– a bit *too* different.'

'Try me,' said Miss Mirabelle.

So Lance perched on the corner of her desk and told Miss Mirabelle his idea. As he explained, a little smile came on to her face for the first time that morning. It grew and grew, like his idea, until it was enormous.

'Brilliant!' she said, when he had finished. 'How did you think of *that*?' She didn't wait

for an answer. 'It is *amazing*,' she said. He could tell from the expression on her face that she was delighted. 'That is –' She paused, searching for the right word, and couldn't find it.

'Different,' she finished up at last. 'That is certainly *different*.'

'Oh yes,' agreed Lance. 'It's different, all right.'

Miss Mirabelle turned to the class.

'We have been saved,' she announced. 'Lance here has had the most brilliant idea.'

Everyone stopped painting to listen. Miss Mirabelle pushed Lance forward.

'Go on,' she ordered. 'Tell everybody.'

So Lance explained his idea a second time. When he had finished there was a long, long silence. The whole class was staring at him. They couldn't believe it. Then, suddenly, someone at the back began to giggle. Just one person at first, and very softly. But soon there was another. And another. And another. And soon the whole class was rocking and

The Country Pancake

laughing, and calling out excitedly.

'It's certainly *different*.'

'There'll be no trouble keeping it a secret. No one would ever dare tell Mrs Spicer!'

'*No one* will want to miss it. *Everyone* will come.'

'We'll make a fortune. Everyone will want a ticket!'

'It's brilliant. *Brilliant*.'

'Why has nobody ever thought of it before?'

'I know why!'

'So do I!'

Miss Mirabelle rose. The silver bell earrings tinkled as she cried out:

'Three cheers for Lancelot Higgins! Hip, hip, *hooray*!'

Mrs Spicer peeped through the little glass pane in the door just as they were cheering their heads off. Nobody even noticed.

'Hip, hip, hooray!'

'Good old Lance!'

'And his amazing cow!'

'Hip, hip, *hooray*.'

Chapter 4

**In which Mrs Spicer sees a Great
Improvement All Round, and is Delighted**

Miss Mirabelle came into school the next
morning with a smile on her face. She reached
in her capacious woven bag and drew out
several balls of knitting wool and a big box of
brand-new ice-lolly sticks.

She laid the balls of wool along the edge of
her desk, and opened the box lid to show them
the lolly sticks packed tightly inside.

'One thousand,' she said. '*Exactly.*'

The Country Pancake

Miss Mirabelle looked round at the sea of baffled faces.

'Now, listen carefully,' she said. 'It's going to be a busy day. Let me explain . . .'

Inside her office, Mrs Spicer sat staring at the sheet of paper on her desk. Printed across the top were the words:

Report on Miss Mirabelle

and nothing else.

Yet . . .

Mrs Spicer was thinking. She was thinking hard. She knew exactly what she thought of Miss Mirabelle. Oh, yes. She knew exactly what she'd like to write. She just wasn't absolutely sure it was quite fair to give anyone, even the amazing Miss Mirabelle, such a terrible report without checking one last time.

She'd creep along. And if Miss Mirabelle was sitting with her head cupped in her hands, staring out of the window while a riot went on around her . . . Or if Miss Mirabelle was peeling an apple with her exquisite pearl knife while everyone watched the skin falling in one long perfect coil . . . Or if there were sniffers in the cupboard . . . Then Mrs Spicer would write her report. Yes! Every last word!

Furtively she tiptoed along the corridor. As she came closer she heard Miss Mirabelle's clear voice echoing from the classroom. But was she teaching them anything? Or was she, as usual, just admiring somebody's wobbly tooth, or showing them photographs of her sister's new-born baby, or asking their advice on the best kitty litter?

But, no! It sounded as if, just for once, she'd actually caught Miss Mirabelle giving a lesson. How very strange!

'If there are twenty-five of you,' Miss Mirabelle was saying, 'And I have exactly one thousand lolly sticks, how many should I give to each of you, to make it fair?'

Miss Mirabelle made it sound as if it really was a problem. What a good way of making division sound interesting – lolly sticks! Mrs

The Country Pancake

Spicer eavesdropped with interest as the whole class struggled aloud with the sum. They all seemed very keen to get it right, as though no one wanted too many, or too few.

Then out the answer popped:

'We get exactly forty each! And there'll be none left over!'

'Good. That will be all fair then,' Miss Mirabelle said. And she sounded as if it really mattered. Mrs Spicer was astonished. She made her way silently back to her office and sat in front of the paper, bewildered. What was she going to do now? She might be a bit of a dragon, but she was always scrupulously fair. She couldn't write a dreadful report on Miss Mirabelle after overhearing that simply splendid lesson in division. She'd have to put the report aside for a little while. Catch Miss Mirabelle out later . . .

Just before break, Mrs Spicer tried again. She slunk along the corridor, making no sound. No sound came from Miss Mirabelle's room, either. Perhaps they were all busy, Mrs

Spicer thought, with one of their little eye-squelching sessions . . .

Mrs Spicer peeped through the pane of glass set in the door. Amazing! She could scarcely believe her eyes! The whole class was working hard, even that little daydreamer, Lancelot Higgins! Everyone's head was bent over their desk. Everyone was concentrating. Usually, when Mrs Spicer peeped into a classroom, at least one person would be staring idly around, and look in her direction, and notice her at once.

Not here. Not today. Today they were all so busy that no one looked up. Mrs Spicer couldn't make out exactly what they were doing. It *looked* as if they were writing numbers neatly on the ends of brand-new lolly sticks, but that was ridiculous. They must have been doing something else. But, no doubt about it, they were certainly working.

Shaking her head in disbelief, Mrs Spicer turned and went back down the corridor. She had better get back to her office. That report

on Miss Mirabelle had to be posted today. But still, it was difficult to write the report she wanted to write after seeing the class working so well and so busily.

It would be better to wait till after break. She'd feel more like it then.

A few minutes after the bell rang to signal the end of break-time, Mrs Spicer pushed aside her coffee cup. Time to write the report! She was just glancing out of the window as she reached for her pen, when she happened to notice the children from Miss Mirabelle's class gathering around the football pitch.

Mrs Spicer studied her watch. Well, really! Break-time ended at least ten minutes ago. What could Miss Mirabelle be thinking of, letting her class wander about all over the place? This would go straight in the report!

But what were they doing? Extraordinary! They were working. No doubt about it. They were working hard. With metre sticks and a long tape-measure, the class was busy measuring along the sides of the football pitch

The Country Pancake

and dividing each side into smaller equal lengths.

Mrs Spicer's writing hand trembled. She had to write the report. She had to write it today. She knew what she wanted to write. She was desperate to write it and get rid of the amazing Miss Mirabelle and her high heels for ever. But what she was seeing outside made it impossible for her to write Miss Mirabelle a bad report. It simply wouldn't be fair. How many teachers can make measuring a rectangle interesting for children? Not very many. Using the football pitch was such a fine idea! Mrs Spicer couldn't help feeling a little bit pleased with Miss Mirabelle as she stared out of the window. She'd have to put off the report till after lunch.

But after lunch things were no worse. In fact, they were even better. Mrs Spicer could scarcely believe it. There were the children from Miss Mirabelle's class, outside again, fanning out along the sides of the football pitch. What did they have in their hands?

Anne Fine

Knitting wool? Yes. How extraordinary! What on earth were they doing?

Mrs Spicer leaned her forehead against the cool glass of her window-pane and watched, fascinated, as the children from Miss Mirabelle's class carefully divided the entire football pitch into exactly equal squares, one thousand of them, and marked them out with wool. Wonderful! The most interesting way of measuring area that Mrs Spicer had ever seen. Why hadn't she thought of teaching it that way herself? Really, she ought to take Miss Mirabelle aside in the staff room next time she saw her and tell her what a splendid idea it was. Excellent! Excellent! So much better than just doing it in the dreary old work books!

And what were they all doing now?

How strange! They were all kneeling down and pushing a little marker like a lolly stick into each square. How clever! Now every square was measured out exactly and marked with one of those numbered lolly sticks. And

there were exactly one thousand!

What a splendid lesson!

Mrs Spicer couldn't help it. When she saw sloppy teaching, she got annoyed. And when she saw splendid teaching, she was delighted. Drawing the sheet of paper towards her, she unscrewed the top of her fountain pen, and wrote.

Report on Miss Mirabelle
I must confess that when Miss Mirabelle first came to teach at Wallisdean Park School I did have doubts. Eye-squelching sessions . . .

Anne Fine

Sniffers in the cupboard . . . And those shoes!
But recently I have seen a great improvement
all round. Not everyone can make an
interesting class out of division, or measuring
rectangles, or working out areas. Mr Rushman
couldn't. Nor could Mrs Maloney or Mr
Hubert. But Miss Mirabelle can. She uses lolly
sticks, and balls of wool – even the football
pitch. She is amazing and I am delighted.
Yours very truly,
Emily Spicer

There. That would do. It was a fine report, and Miss Mirabelle deserved it. Yes! Every last word!

Mrs Spicer folded the sheet of paper, slid it inside the envelope and sealed the flap. She glanced at her watch again. Time for the post.

She walked towards the door, holding the letter in her hand. And for the first time ever when thinking about Miss Mirabelle, Mrs Spicer was smiling. A little melody she'd overheard the children singing in the

54

The Country Pancake

playground floated into her mind, and she began to hum. What were the words?

Which would you rather?
Run a mile?
Jump a stile?
Or eat a country pancake?

Really it was a very sweet little song, compared with a lot of the rather tasteless rubbish one heard them bellowing at playtime. Mrs Spicer sang it to herself all the way home and for most of the evening.

Chapter 5

**In which Lance's Granny is
Totally Disgusted**

The farmer was astonished. She dropped the
end of the hosepipe she was dragging across
the courtyard and stared at Lance.

'You want to borrow a *cow*?'

Lance stared at the water scudding in silky
waves across the cobbles.

'Yes, please,' he answered politely. 'Just for
the afternoon. She'll be back in time for
milking.'

'A *cow*,' said the farmer meditatively. 'Fancy

The Country Pancake

a cow! I'm often asked for a horse. Never a cow.'

'Well,' Lance said, a shade uneasily. 'This is a bit different.'

'It certainly is,' said the farmer. 'What do you want a cow for?'

Lance looked down and inspected the ends of his shoes. They were muddy from the water spilling out of the hosepipe. This was the moment he'd been dreading. It hadn't been too bad, whispering the idea into Miss Mirabelle's ear in the classroom. That hadn't been too difficult. And it hadn't been all that hard, either, explaining it to everyone else in the class. They'd just sat wide-eyed, listening quietly (until the giggling began, of course).

Telling the farmer was not quite so easy. Lance found it impossible to describe exactly why he wanted to borrow a cow.

'Oh, just to sort of walk about a bit.'

'Just sort of walk about a bit?'

'Yes. On our school football pitch.'

The farmer was mystified.

'But what's the *point*?'

Lance gave up inspecting the ends of his shoes and took to inspecting his fingernails instead.

'People will probably be standing around the pitch,' he offered finally, after a long struggle for words. 'Sort of watching.'

'Sort of watching? Sort of watching *what*?'

'The cow.'

'But *why*?'

Lance shrugged, as if that part of things were no concern of his.

'Well, really, just to see where she goes, I expect.'

The farmer shook her head.

'I don't know,' she said. 'I'm glad I don't have any children. I'm sure I'd worry myself silly about what they do all day in school.'

She reached down for the end of her hosepipe.

'Well, Lance,' she said, 'you've spent whole weeks helping me. So you can borrow a cow for one afternoon. But it will have to be

The Country Pancake

Flossie. Flossie knows you, and Flossie is calm and sensible. Flossie won't mind.'

'I'm sure no cow would *mind*,' Lance said eagerly. 'Our football pitch must be like Sunday dinner to a cow. All lovely and rich and green and luscious.'

'I can't think why you want a cow wandering about on it, then,' said the farmer. 'Before you know where you are, you'll be having to run after her with a shovel!'

She took off to the barn, dragging the hose. If she'd looked back, she might have seen Lance standing there in the courtyard hugging himself and grinning, before he too took off towards the meadow.

Flossie was lying in the meadow, chewing the cud. Lance slipped through the bars of the fence and strode over towards her. Most of the other cows in the herd got up and walked away as he came closer, but Flossie didn't bother.

Lance sat cross-legged on the grass in front

of her.

'Hello, Flossie.'

Chewing, she gazed into his eyes. He gazed back into hers. They were enormous, as dark and gleaming as the beautiful old polished furniture in Granny's house.

'Flossie,' said Lance. 'It's about Saturday.'

He'd known her all her life. He loved her dearly. He couldn't just spring this on her. He had to explain.

'The thing is,' said Lance, 'I need your help.'

Flossie kept chewing, imperturbably.

Lance spread his hands.

'It's an odd thing to ask anyone to do,' he admitted openly. 'Even a cow.'

Her great jaws ground away steadily at the green spinachy cud. She didn't seem at all bothered.

'I wouldn't ask you if I had a choice,' said Lance. 'To be honest, I wish she'd picked another cow entirely. I wish she hadn't chosen you. But she says you're calm and sensible . . .'

He watched her closely.

'And she says you won't mind.'

Flossie swung her great head round and stared out thoughtfully over the meadow. Lance wondered what she was thinking. What did cows think about? Did cows think at all?

Not really, he decided. They couldn't think like people can. Oh, they could feel. They could feel pain if they got a thorn impacted in one of their hooves, or if nobody milked them, or if they broke a leg.

And they could feel satisfaction if they had a long drink of water on a hot day, or found a good bit of fence to scratch on.

And they could follow their instincts enough to gather at the corner of the field when it was milking time, and find their way to their own stalls.

But Flossie couldn't think the same way Lance could think. And she couldn't have such complicated feelings. She wouldn't feel excited about something that was going to happen, and she wouldn't fret afterwards if it went wrong. Cows had no imagination. That's why they were so peaceful, Lance thought. They didn't spend their days, like he did, chewing over yesterday and tomorrow. They just chewed the cud.

It was a pretty cushy life, when you came to think about it. No worries. Water on tap. Salt-licks tied to the fence. Constant meals. Nice warm barn. No fears for the future. No reason why a cow shouldn't be expected to be a bit of a help every now and again, when opportunity offered.

Lance rose to his feet, decided.

The Country Pancake

'So you'll help, won't you, Flossie? You won't mind?'

Flossie burped contentedly. The sweet smell of fermenting cud wafted over Lance. He waved it away.

Flossie struggled to her feet, startled.

'Don't bother to get up,' said Lance. 'I'm leaving anyway. But I'll be back to fetch you on Saturday.'

He paused, still a tiny bit anxious about the arrangement. There was one more small thing he felt he really should get clear.

'I do hope you understand how serious all this is,' he said gravely to Flossie. 'Almost all of the squares of the football pitch have been bought in the raffle. So we *must* have a winner.' He caught Flossie's eye. 'You mustn't just come and wander round the football pitch and nothing else. You mustn't let me down.'

As if deeply offended at the very suggestion that she might fail in her charitable duty, Flossie swung round, turning her back on him. Delicately raising her tail, she left a huge fresh deposit practically at his feet before indifferently ambling off.

Lance looked down at the great steaming pancake, two inches from his shoes. Then he looked up and grinned. And calling after Flossie who was disappearing between the trees, he added his last stern warning:

'Mind now, Flossie! I'm taking that as a definite *promise*!'

'A raffle!' said Granny. 'Lovely. I adore raffles. May I buy a ticket?'

Lance dug in his pocket and drew out the last of the lolly sticks. They had been selling like hot cakes all week.

'Here,' he said. 'I saved the last five for you. Fifty pence each.'

Granny took the lolly sticks and inspected them curiously.

'A bit odd,' she said. 'Not like your common or garden raffle ticket.'

'They stick in the ground well,' Lance assured her.

The Country Pancake

Granny found herself eyeing Lance rather carefully.

'I'm glad your term is nearly over,' she said. 'Sometimes I worry that school is all too much for you.'

Lance couldn't think what she was on about. He carried on explaining about the lolly sticks.

'They have to stick in the ground,' he said. 'To mark the raffle squares. We read the number on the lolly stick when Flossie has chosen.'

'Flossie?'

'You know Flossie,' Lance said. 'Flossie the cow.'

Granny narrowed her eyes.

'A cow is picking the winner? A *cow*?'

'Yes,' Lance said. 'It's all arranged. It was my idea.'

Granny reached out a hand and laid it thoughtfully on Lance's forehead.

'I'm wondering if I should take you home,' she said. 'I'm not absolutely one hundred per cent certain you ought to be out of bed.'

Lance realised suddenly that Granny thought he was unhinged.

'I'm perfectly all right,' he assured her. 'I haven't gone potty. Flossie will choose the winner.'

'Oh yes? Is she going to dip her hoof in a tub?'

'Of course not,' said Lance. 'She's going to do it differently. She's going to –'

He broke off. However many times he tried to describe the process, this bit was always difficult. He had no trouble imagining it himself. In his own mind the picture was perfectly clear. It was like one of his daydreams. Flossie became as sleek and powerful as the most valuable Arabian mare. She wore a bridle studded with precious jewels that glittered fiercely in the harsh sunlight. Astride her rode Lance himself, high in the saddle. He wore a suit of the richest velvet, a cap with a feather and a silver sword. Upon his saddle was emblazoned the royal crest that

The Country Pancake

proclaimed his princely ancestry.

Tall, noble, handsome . . . When he rode through the gate into the field the crowds went mad, cheering wildly, hurling their hats in the air, dropping to their knees in wonder, fainting from the sheer excitement of the day.

Three times around the field of green they rode, he and Flossie, until at last the waiting crowd fell silent, gasped –

'Lance?'

Granny was looking quite anxious.

'Lance? Are you all right, dear?'

Lance pulled himself together.

'Sorry. I was just off in a daydream.'

Hastily Granny gathered up her jacket and her bag. She had decided it was best to take her grandson home and leave him in his parents' care. Obviously he was a bit feverish.

As they walked down the lane, hand in hand, the sight of all the cows in the meadow reminded Granny of what they had been talking about before Lance suddenly went peculiar.

'About this raffle, Lance. Explain to me again. How is the cow going to pick the winner?'

Lance tried to pick his words carefully. But it was no use. Granny stopped dead in her tracks.

'Lancelot Higgins! I am totally *disgusted*!'

Furiously blushing, Lance stared ahead.

All the way home, Granny went on about it. 'Disgraceful . . . don't know what the schools are coming to . . . read in the papers . . . I blame the teachers, frankly . . . wouldn't dream of such a thing in my day . . . totally disgusted.'

Lance just kept walking.

As they reached the front gate, Granny stopped muttering and laid her hand on his.

'I won't come in. I'll say goodbye here.'

Lance hung his head.

Granny lifted his chin.

'Lance? Haven't you forgotten something?'

Dutifully, he raised himself on tiptoes, to be kissed.

The Country Pancake

'No, not that,' Granny said impatiently. 'You've forgotten to give me my lolly sticks for the raffle.'

Lance stared.

'But I thought that you were totally disgusted!'

Now it was Lance's Granny's turn to blush.

'And so I am. But I'm not going to miss a good raffle.'

A little shyly, Lance dug in his pockets and drew out the five lolly sticks he had so

carefully saved for her all week.

Shyly, Granny dug in her purse and gave him the money.

'There,' she said. 'Wish me luck.'

'Good luck.'

Granny kissed him again, properly this time.

'You, too,' she laughed. 'You may need all the luck that you can get. What will you do if Flossie lets you down?'

Lance grinned.

'I don't know,' he teased. 'Run a mile? Jump a stile?'

Before she could reach out to put her hand over his mouth and stop him finishing the rhyme, he was safely up the path.

Chapter 6

**In which we all
watch Dear Flossie
Save the Day**

The farmer led Flossie out of the barn.
Around her neck was a silken red cord with a
tassel at each end.

'It's my dressing-gown belt,' said the farmer.
'I thought you'd like Flossie to look nice for
the occasion.'

'She looks beautiful,' Lance said. 'She
always does.'

Flossie tossed her head proudly.

'Off we go, then,' said the farmer. She slapped Flossie's rump hard. Not a speck of dust flew up.

'You've groomed her!' cried Lance.

The farmer shrugged.

'Flossie's big day,' she said, lifting the gate latch. 'And I must say I shall be glad when it's over. An awful lot of people seem to have chosen this week to stroll up my lane and have a good peer in my meadow.'

'What on earth for?'

'Search me. But I bet you have quite a few dung-pat experts watching this raffle.'

She watched as Lance led Flossie carefully into the lane. She followed a few yards behind, ready to warn any traffic to slow down, but no cars came along before Lance reached the fork in the lane and turned down the narrow path that led to the football pitch.

So many people! Milling everywhere! It seemed as if everyone in the village had come along to Open Day, and brought all their friends. Even as he watched, more people spilled out of the school hall, after the end of the show. The Bring and buy stall was practically sold out already. The Sponsored Runners were just running back. Even the Infants had stopped collecting in their Spaceman Snoopy boxes, for fear the weight of cash inside would damage them.

Suddenly Lance and Flossie were spotted.

'There's the cow!'

'Raffle time!'

Everyone gathered around the edge of the football pitch, some frantically searching their pockets for lolly sticks, some brandishing lucky mascots, some loudly admiring Flossie's fancy leading rein.

'Just what I need for my dressing-gown,' said Old Mr Hogg as soon as he saw it. 'Do you suppose I could get one from an agricultural supplier?'

Lance looked around. Had *everyone* bought a lolly stick? There was Mrs Spicer, clutching a handful and looking a little bemused. There beside her was Miss Mirabelle, holding a few more and looking striking in a slinky black dress. There was the janitor, and the school governors. And Granny in the corner, waving excitedly. And his parents behind her.

Lance took a few steps forward. Tugging a little on the silken cord, Flossie followed.

The whispers ran around the football pitch –

'Keep your voices down!'

'Hush, now!'

'Mustn't worry the cow!'

– until there was absolute quiet.

Lance's big moment. He mustn't muff it now. This was the stuff of his daydreams – the time when, with grace and skill and dignity, he would lead Flossie out on to the football pitch to launch his extraordinary raffle. It was everything he dreamed about. It was exotic. It was different. It was –

Why was Deborah running up to him, while everyone watched?

'Here,' she said, her clear voice carrying easily the entire length of the pitch. 'Miss Mirabelle said I was to give you this.'

The Country Pancake

It was a shovel. A great big rusty-edged shovel. Not different. Not exotic. Not at all the stuff of daydreams.

'Thank you,' said Lance. (His voice was frosty cold.)

'Go *on*, then,' said Deborah. '*Take* it. It's *heavy*.

Lance had no choice. He had to take it. And he could not walk Flossie back to the edge of the pitch, to dump it neatly out of sight between the bystanders' legs. He was just stuck with it.

And that's how it came about that the famous photograph of Lancelot Higgins that everyone saw in their newspapers the next morning showed him leading his cow so proudly into the middle of the football pitch waving a shovel to the cheering crowds.

'Let her go!'

'Take off the leading rein!'

'Leave her to wander!'

Lance tugged at the knot in the dressing-gown cord. It slid undone. He pulled the cord

over Flossie's huge head.

Flossie mooed softly, and butted Lance gently in the belly with her head.

Lance leaned forward and tickled her behind both ears.

'Off you go, Flossie,' he whispered. 'Sunday lunch one day early. Eat up. Feel free to go anywhere you want, do whatever you feel like doing. Make yourself at home.'

He added one last little plea.

The Country Pancake

'And don't let me down!'

Then he took off for the edge of the pitch, for fear that the crowd would accuse him of cheating.

Flossie looked round. People. She wasn't interested in people. She looked down. Grass. Oh, she was interested in grass. It had a few funny little wooden sticks poking up out of it, but they didn't bother her. It was fine grass, and ripe for chewing.

Keeping her eyes forever on the move for the next good patch, Flossie moved off across the football pitch.

Around the edge a hundred conversations took up again softly.

'How much is the prize?'

'Fifty pounds!'

'One thousand squares, though. At fifty pence a square. Why, that's –'

The crowd struggled with the sum.

Mrs Spicer was first.

'Why!' she declared to Miss Mirabelle. 'That's five hundred pounds!'

Anne Fine

Miss Mirabelle was busy struggling with her high heels which kept sinking deeply into the soft ground, making her look rather unbalanced and peculiar.

'What?' she said. 'Oh yes. That's right. Fifty pounds for the winner, and the rest for the school.'

Mrs Spicer was thrilled.

'Four hundred and fifty pounds!' she repeated. 'I could buy all those new maths books!'

Miss Mirabelle made a little face.

Mrs Spicer was quite excited now.

'And what exactly is the cow going to do, to choose the winning square?'

Perhaps Miss Mirabelle, struggling with her disappearing heels, did not take quite the care she ought to have done to choose her words.

'Flossie? Oh, she's just supposed to drop a giant pancake.'

'Drop a giant pancake?'

'That's right.'

Mrs Spicer was appalled. Truly appalled.

The Country Pancake

People who eavesdropped offered the opinion quite freely afterwards that, had she suffered from a weak heart, she might have died on the spot.

But Miss Mirabelle, still hauling her heels out of the mud, was paying no attention to the look on Mrs Spicer's face.

'Let's just hope the whole lot plops straight on one square,' she was saying. 'I can't imagine the trouble we'll have if it spreads over several. People will want us to weigh it, I shouldn't wonder, to get their fair share of the prize money.'

As one heel shot out of the mud without warning, the other sank deeply in again.

'I've done my best,' Miss Mirabelle went on irritably. 'Brushed up on proportion in the maths books, and given Lance a shovel.'

'A shovel . . .'

Mrs Spicer felt faint. Could all these people – even the governors! – be standing here waiting to see where a cow –

Oh, it didn't bear thinking about! Mrs

Spicer's voice was thick with danger as she asked Miss Mirabelle:

'And may I ask, dear, whose idea this is?'

There! Both heels out at last! Miss Mirabelle looked up. Mrs Spicer was staring at her with hostile, beady eyes. Her face was quite ashen. Was the old dragon annoyed? Really, some people were impossible to please. Four hundred and fifty pounds in the school's pocket, and she was fussing about a little cowpat!

Better not get poor little Lancelot Higgins in trouble, though. He'd been a poppet, and worked so hard. The very last thing Miss Mirabelle wanted was to reward him with a great row from Mrs Spicer.

She'd better take the blame herself.

'Oh, this whole raffle was all my idea.'

Behind her she thought she heard a little gasp of shock. She spun around. Lance Higgins was staring at her, open-mouthed. She was about to give him a little nudge and a wink, to try to explain to him why she had

Anne Fine

taken it upon herself to claim his brilliant idea for her own, when, all round the pitch, there was a sudden ripple of excitement.

Forgetting Lance, Miss Mirabelle turned back to see what was happening.

Oh, good old Flossie! She was coming up trumps! Head in the wind, tail raised triumphant, she was picking a winner!

'Hurrah!'

'Yippee!'

'Well done, Flossie! Well done!'

The crowd roared its approval. A dozen people ran across the pitch to check the lolly stick that marked the square.

'Four hundred and twelve!'

Waves of excitement ran around the pitch, as everyone checked their own lolly sticks, and those of their neighbours.

'Old Mr Hogg!'

'The winner!'

'No need to go searching for a new cord now, eh, Hogg? Get yourself a brand-new dressing-gown!'

The Country Pancake

Old Mr Hogg stumbled forward. Before Mrs Spicer realised what was happening, Miss Mirabelle had thrust a fifty pound note into her hand.

'The presentation!'

'Speech! Speech!'

'Vote of thanks!'

Lance didn't stay to hear any speeches. Or any votes of thanks. Or any more hurrahs. He didn't stay to clear up after Flossie with the shovel, either. If this whole raffle was all her idea, then let Miss Mirabelle shovel up the cowpat!

He was *finished* with Miss Mirabelle anyway. She might still be better than the terrifying Mr Rushman, or the boring Mrs Maloney, or the dreadful Mr Hubert; but she was a bit *too* amazing for Lancelot Higgins.

Stealing his idea! What an exotic *cheek*!

Lance crept away, past Granny telling the governors how shocked she was by modern teaching methods. (She'd have been singing a very different tune, he knew, if she'd won the raffle.) He went past the janitor, and threaded his way between other people's parents, until he found himself beside the farmer, who was tethering Flossie.

'Can I walk her home?'

'Oh please, Lance. I should get back to work.'

This time she went ahead, to warn the traffic. Lance strolled behind, with Flossie. He didn't want to be a wet blanket and spoil her big day, but he couldn't help telling her what he was thinking.

'I'm *finished* with Miss Mirabelle. She's on her own now. She can look after herself. She can right her own wrongs, and kill her own dragons, and get her own damselly self out of her own distress.'

Flossie mooed sympathy and agreement as she clopped along.

'Cheek!' Lance was muttering, patting her neck for comfort. 'What is so special about Miss Mirabelle anyway? That's what I'd like to know. She isn't all *that* amazing. Anyone

The Country Pancake

can wear fancy clothes and peel a silly apple.
Anyone can start up a Sing Song. No one can
stand sniffers. And it's just plain stupid to try
walking in high heels around a football pitch!'

He stopped at the gate and looked deep into
Flossie's beautiful velvet eyes.

'You're not exotic,' he confessed. 'You're not
different. You don't promise adventure. Let's
face it, Flossie, you're not even very bright.
But I can tell all my troubles to you. And I
love you dearly. You're more amazing than

Miss Mirabelle any day. And you make really good country pancakes!'

Pleased to be back with the herd, Flossie trotted off into the meadow, tossing her head.

Pleased to be nearly home, Lancelot followed her.

BiLL'S NEW FROCK

Bill Simpson wakes up to find he's a girl, and, worse, his mother makes him wear a frilly pink dress to school. How on earth is he going to survive a whole day like this?

Everything just seems to be *different* for girls . . .

'Stylishly written and thought-provoking' *Guardian*

'. . . a gem. Don't miss it.' *TES*

WINNER OF THE SMARTIES PRIZE

How To Write rEally BAdLy

Chester Howard can see Joe's project 'How to Write Neatly' can only be a disaster. Bottom of the class, Joe makes a terrible mess of his work, jumbling letters and numbers up together.

But a project called 'How to Write Really Badly' – now there's something Joe can do better than anyone else.

And Chester is about to find there's a lot more to Joe than he expected . . .

'Screamingly funny' *The Herald*

'Fine has a rare genius for building a funny, enriching and moving story around the nuts and bolts of school life' *The Times*

WINNER OF THE *TES* NASEN AWARD

'The chicken gave it to me'

Gemma doesn't believe a chicken could have written a book – chickens can't even read! But here in front of them is *The True Story of Harrowing Farm*, and its scratchy pages definitely look, well, *chickeny*.

It is an epic tale of cruelty and bravery, the story of a chicken who flies frillions of miles, reaching the heights of intergalactic superstardom, to try to save us humans . . .

'a clever and biting social fable . . . wit and brilliance sparkle on every page.' *Junior Bookshelf*

'a terrific little book . . .' Joanna Lumley

Anne Fine has won many awards, including the Carnegie Medal and Whitbread Children's Award twice each, the Guardian Children's Fiction Award and the Smarties Prize.